Evening Class

MAEVE BINCHY

Level 4

Retold by Evadne Adrian-Vallance
Series Editors: Andy Hopkins and Jocelyn Potter

Pearson Education Limited
Edinburgh Gate, Harlow,
Essex CM20 2JE, England
and Associated Companies throughout the world.

ISBN 0 582 27849 X

First published in Great Britain by Orion 1996
This edition first published 2000

Second impression 2000

Original copyright © Maeve Binchy 1996
Text copyright © Penguin Books 2000
Illustrations copyright © David Cuzik (Pennant) 2000
All rights reserved

Typeset by Digital Type, London
Set in 11/14pt Bembo
Printed in Spain by Mateu Cromo, S. A. Pinto (Madrid)

Published by Pearson Education Limited in association with
Penguin Books Ltd, both companies being subsidiaries of Pearson Plc

For a complete list of the titles available in the Penguin Readers series please write to your local
Pearson Education office or to: Marketing Department, Penguin Longman Publishing,
5 Bentinck Street, London W1M 5RN.

Contents

Introduction

These thirty people really believed that they were going on a trip to Rome. Tony O'Brien, who was a strong man, felt slightly weak at the thought.

A mixed group of people all have their own reasons for joining the new Italian evening class in Dublin. Bill wants to improve his chances at work; Lou has criminal intentions; Connie needs an escape from her unhappy home life, and Laddy believes that he has been invited to Italy. The classes have been organized by two people with empty, lonely lives: the schoolteacher Aidan Dunne, and Nora O'Donaghue, who everybody knows as Signora. Like the other members of the group, their lives are changed for ever as the story develops.

Maeve Binchy was born in 1940 and grew up in County Dublin in Ireland. After a short time as a teacher, she found work writing for the *Irish Times* and moved to London. She had great success with her early plays and collections of short stories but her first full-length book, *Light a Penny Candle*, did not appear until 1982. It was an immediate success and since that time Binchy has become one of Ireland's best-known writers.

Her other books include *Echoes* (1985*)*, *Firefly Summer* (1987), *Circle of Friends* (1990), *The Copper Beech* (1992) and *The Glass Lake* (1994).

Chapter 1   Aidan

There was a time when their marriage had been good. They looked happy in their old photographs. But that was long ago now, perhaps fifteen years.

So what had gone wrong? They hadn't argued. There had been no other women in Aidan's life. Nell was an attractive woman but he felt sure that she had not had relationships with other men. No, he decided, he and Nell had just become different people over the years.

Nell hadn't asked about his work for a long time now. He made a great effort to take an interest in her life. But she never talked about Quentin's, the restaurant where she worked at the cash desk. It was just a job, she said. He had no more success with his daughters.

Grania, now twenty-one, worked in a bank but she didn't want to discuss it. And it was the same with nineteen-year-old Brigid. 'The shop's fine, Dad,' she said.

Sometimes he thought that things might get better when he became Principal at the school. But another man, also in his forties, might get the job. This was Tony O'Brien, who never stayed late or took part in the life of the school as Aidan did. Tony O'Brien smoked in front of the children, had lunch in a bar and was often seen with younger women. They couldn't seriously want him for the job, could they?

Sundays were the days that Aidan found the hardest. In the past, the whole family had gone to the country or the sea for the day. But now the girls watched television, washed their hair and clothes and spoke to friends on the telephone. Nell usually went somewhere to meet a friend. On Sundays, Aidan felt that he really wasn't noticed in his own home.

Once or twice recently, Nell had suggested that Aidan could make their guest room into a study for himself. They never had any guests. But Aidan felt that, shut in his study, all communication with his family might finally end.

◆

'Did you have a good weekend?' Tony O'Brien asked in the teachers' room on Monday morning.

'Quiet, you know,' Aidan answered.

'Oh, well, lucky you. I was at a party last night and I'm suffering from it,' Tony complained. 'Oh, and I met someone who knew you.'

'At a party? I doubt that,' Aidan smiled.

'No, really, she did. When I told her I taught here, she asked if I knew you.'

'And who was she?' Aidan was interested now.

'I didn't get her name. Nice girl.'

Aidan watched as Tony O'Brien went into his class. His pupils became silent immediately. Aidan couldn't understand why these sixteen-year-old boys and girls liked Tony so much. The man didn't even remember their names.

Aidan went into his own class and waited at the door while his pupils slowly stopped making a noise. Had Mr Walsh, the old Principal, passed behind him while he was waiting? It didn't matter. Aidan was the most responsible teacher in Mountainview. Everyone knew that.

◆

That afternoon, Mr Walsh called Aidan into his office.

'You and I feel the same about a lot of things, Aidan,' he said. 'And if I had a vote, you would be in my job in September.'

'Thank you, Mr Walsh. That's very good to know.'

'There's nothing to thank me for. The Principal doesn't have a vote so I can't do anything for you. That's what I'm trying to tell you. Of course, I might be wrong. You might still get the job, but it's not the end of the world you know, if you don't. You're a family man – lots of life at home.'

Aidan tried not to show what he was feeling. 'Yes, of course, you're quite right,' he said.

'But?' the older man asked kindly.

Aidan chose his words with care. 'It's not the end of the world, but I had hoped that it might be a new beginning. I'm like you – you know, married to Mountainview.'

'I know you are,' said Mr Walsh, gently. Outside the room were the noises of a school at four-thirty in the afternoon – bells ringing, children shouting. It was all so safe, so familiar. 'Tony O'Brien seems to be the one they want. Nothing definite yet, not until next week. But they seem to think he's the man for the times that we live in. A strong man to solve difficult problems. But you've got a wife and daughters, Aidan. You should build on that.'

♦

At home, Aidan found Nell in the black dress she wore for work in the restaurant.

'But you don't work Monday nights,' he cried.

'They needed more people, and I thought why not, there's nothing on television,' she said.

'Oh, I see,' he said. 'Are the girls home?'

'Grania's in the bathroom. She's meeting someone special tonight, it seems. I've left you some food on the kitchen table. See you later.' And she was gone.

Aidan made himself a cup of coffee and went into the guest room, closing the door behind him. Perhaps he should make this room into his own place, as Nell had suggested. He realized now that his family life had ended. And he would not be married to Mountainview either.

He started to plan it. He had seen an old desk that he liked, and he would have fresh flowers in the room. There would be a wall with books on it and he'd put up Italian pictures. He loved

Italy. He and Nell had gone there on holiday when they were first married.

There was a knock on the door. Grania stood there, dressed for her evening out. 'Are you all right, Daddy?'

'I'm fine,' he said. He tried to smile. 'Are you going somewhere nice?'

'I don't know. I've met someone I like a lot, but listen, I'll tell you about it some other time.'

He felt so sad. She wanted to get away. 'That's fine,' he said. 'Enjoy your evening.'

Aidan was in bed when Nell came home at one o'clock. She climbed in on her side of the bed, as far from him as possible. Grania still wasn't home. The girls came and went when they wanted to. So he was pleased when he heard the hall door open and her footsteps on the stairs.

'Nice evening, Grania?' Aidan asked at breakfast.

'Yes, OK.'

'Good. Was it busy in the restaurant?' he asked Nell.

'Quite busy for a Monday,' she said. She spoke in the way she would speak to someone she had met on a bus.

Aidan took his case and left for school. When he got there, Tony O'Brien was taking something for a headache.

'I'm getting too old for these late nights,' he said.

'Did you enjoy it – I mean, the late night?'

'Well, I was with a nice girl, but I still have to face my class today.'

◆

The day passed as days always pass, and the next and the next. Aidan hadn't forgotten his study. He began to collect little bits of his dream: a low table for near the window, a big chair. And one day he would get some material to cover the chair: something in gold or yellow, something bright.

'Have you heard anything about the big job at the school?'

4

'Have you heard anything about the big job at the school?'

Nell asked to his surprise one evening, when they were all in the kitchen.

He lied. 'Nothing. But they're voting on it next week.'

'You'll get it. Old Walsh loves the ground you walk on,' Nell said.

'He doesn't have a vote, actually, so that doesn't help me.' Aidan gave a nervous laugh.

'But who would they have if they didn't have you?' Grania wanted to know.

'How should I know? Someone from outside . . . , or someone from inside that we haven't thought of.'

'But you do think you'll get it, don't you?' Nell said.

Aidan pretended to feel confident. 'Of course I will.'

◆

It was their sixth evening out together. Grania really liked him. He was more interesting than people of her own age.

There was only one problem. Tony worked at Dad's school. The very first time she met him, she had asked him if he knew Aidan Dunne. But she hadn't told Dad about Tony yet. She would tell him if the relationship developed. And Tony would have to be even nicer to her if she was the Principal's daughter!

◆

Tony sat at the bar, smoking. He would have to smoke less when he was Principal. But it wasn't a big price to pay for a good job. Of course, nobody else knew that they had offered him the job. It was still a secret.

Other things were going well for him too. Grania was warm and generous, quite special. She was only twenty-one, less than half his age, but that needn't be a big problem.

He saw her come into the bar and he felt happy.

'You look beautiful,' he said.

They talked and drank together for a time, laughing and happily exchanging news.

'Well, there are lots of places we could go this evening,' Tony said. 'Or shall I cook for you at home?'

'Thank you, Tony,' Grania said. 'I'd like that.'

'More wine?' Tony asked Grania later that evening.

'No, I must go, Tony ... I've got to get to the bank in the morning and you've got to get to Mountainview.'

'Oh, that doesn't matter.' He didn't want her to go.

Grania laughed. 'You won't say that to me next term. My father's going to be Principal of Mountainview.'

'Your father's going to be *what*?'

'Principal. It's a secret until next week, but I think everyone expects it.'

'What's your father's name?'

'Dunne, like mine. Aidan Dunne.'

'Oh my God,' said Tony O'Brien. 'He told you this?' He took both Grania's hands in his. 'This is the most important thing I have ever said in my life, Grania. You mustn't tell your father that you've been meeting me. We'll tell him that later. But there's something I have to tell him first.'

'Tell me,' she said.

'I can't. But you must believe that I want the very best for you. If you care about me, just wait a day or two.'

◆

'Aidan, I need to talk to you this minute,' Tony O'Brien said, when he found him at school.

'Can't it wait until after school, Tony ...?'

'No, now. Let's go somewhere quiet,' Tony said, almost pulling Aidan with him. 'Aidan.' Tony O'Brien's voice had changed. 'Aidan, I'm going to be the Principal. They were going to announce it next week, but I think it's better if I make them do it today.'

'What ... why?' Aidan felt he had been hit in the stomach.

'So that you stop believing that you're going to get the job

. . . upsetting yourself, upsetting other people . . . that's why. We all thought that Walsh had told you.'

'He only said that you might get the job, and that he would be sorry if you did.'

'Aidan, the job of Principal is changing. They don't want someone nice. They want someone who's not afraid to argue with the Department of Education. But I'm going to need you, Aidan, to help me. The school needs you.'

'No, I couldn't stay here with you as Principal. I don't even think you're a good teacher. And I'd feel embarrassed. My family think the job's mine. They're waiting to celebrate.'

'Then give them something to celebrate.'

'Like what, for example?'

'Imagine that you could have another position in the school. Something new . . . what would you like to do?'

'Look, I know you're trying to help, Tony, but it's not what I need at the moment . . .'

'I'm the Principal. I can do what I want. I want you with me here. So, tell me what you would do here, if you could.'

'Well, I know you won't like it, because it's not really for the school. But I think we should have evening classes.'

'What? What kind of evening classes?'

The announcements were made that afternoon: Adult Education classes would begin in September, organized by Aidan Dunne. The new Principal would be Tony O'Brien.

Later, as Aidan walked out of the school gate, he looked at the school building where he and Tony had decided to hold the evening classes. It had its own entrance and two big classrooms. It would be perfect.

◆

'I have very good news,' Aidan said to his family at supper. He told them all about the evening classes and that he would start with Italian.

They seemed pleased and asked him a lot of questions. He was already making plans. He would put pictures and maps of Italy all over the walls; they might do some Italian cooking or listen to Italian music; he could ask people with a knowledge of Italy to give talks.

'But won't you find this a lot of work as well as being Principal?' Nell asked.

'Oh no, I'm doing it instead of being Principal,' he explained and looked at their faces. Nobody seemed surprised. They continued talking like a real family.

Later Brigid asked: 'Who will become Principal now, if you're not going to do it?'

'Oh, a teacher called Tony O'Brien. He's a good man; he'll be all right for Mountainview.'

He poured them another glass of wine from the bottle he had bought to celebrate. They didn't notice Grania as she got up and quietly left the room.

♦

Tony O'Brien sat in his sitting-room and waited for Grania. She would have to come. Then the doorbell rang and she stood there, eyes red from crying.

She walked into the room, young but not confident now. 'You've been laughing at me all the time, laughing at my father. I hope that this is the worst thing that will ever happen to me ...'

'This morning I didn't know you were Aidan Dunne's daughter. And I didn't know that Aidan thought he would be Principal.'

'Why didn't you tell me you'd got the job?' she cried.

'Because I had to tell your father first. And I wanted him to get what he wanted too ... a new position.'

'You've made my father and me look stupid. I don't think I ever want to see you again.'

'I hope that's not true. I'm very, very fond of you, Grania.'

9

They looked at each other for a few minutes. Then he spoke again. 'Give it some time, Grania. Think about it. You'll soon know how you really feel about me. But you know how *I* feel.'

'I don't think I'll be back.'

'Let's agree never to say never,' he smiled.

He stood at the doorway as she walked down the road. Would she ever come back? He didn't know. But he felt more hopeful about that than he did about the evening classes.

Chapter 2   Signora

For years when Nora O'Donaghue lived in Sicily, she had received no letter from home. Of course, her parents couldn't forgive her for loving Mario. They were upset that she had followed him to his small village in Sicily.

She had first known Mario when she was working in London, and she had been his red-haired princess, the most beautiful girl in the world. But in the end he had gone home to marry Gabriella. 'My family want this marriage very much,' he had said, 'and her family also want it. We are Sicilians; we must listen to our families.'

But Nora couldn't let him go. She didn't like to remember Mario's anger when she got off the bus in Annunziata, outside the hotel that he owned. 'You are making things very difficult for me,' he had said.

'But I love you,' Nora had replied. 'And you love me. I have to be where you are. I will stay here always.'

The years had passed and Signora,★ as they had called her in Annunziata, had become part of the life there. She lived in two rooms in a house on the square. Her rent was low as she helped

★ Signora: the Italian word for *madam*.

10

to look after the old people who owned the house. She made a little money by teaching English in the school every Friday morning and taking tourists round the church. She sewed a little and took what she made to a big town to sell.

And she loved every stone of the place because it was where Mario lived and worked. She watched him marry Gabriella and she watched his sons and daughters grow up. It was enough that he smiled up at her as she sat sewing in her window.

Signora realized that many of the men in Annunziata knew that there was a relationship between Mario and her. But it didn't worry them; it made Mario more of a man in their eyes. She always believed that the women knew nothing of their love, their meetings. They smiled at her over the long years as she slowly learnt their language. They stopped asking her when she was going home. She wasn't upsetting anyone. She could stay.

♦

Signora's red hair began to go a little grey as her fiftieth birthday came near. But unlike the dark women around her, it didn't seem to age her. Probably Mario had got older too but she didn't notice it.

Signora always slept with her window on the square slightly open, so she was one of the first to hear the noise when Gabriella's brothers went to wake the doctor. Signora stood in the shadows and watched. There had been an accident, that was clear. Please God, not one of their children, she thought.

And then she saw Gabriella on the doorstep. She was holding her face in her hands and her cries went up into the mountains around Annunziata: 'MARIO, MARIO . . .'

The sound came into Signora's bedroom, and her heart stopped as she watched them lift the body out of the car. She went down to the square. It was full of his family, neighbours and friends. It seemed he had been driving home from another village. He had missed a corner and the car had turned over many times. She had to see him, to touch his face. But hands reached out to her and pulled her back. Gabriella's brothers didn't want the whole village to see her crying, showing her love.

He was dead, and they all seemed to think that she would now leave. But Signora had lived there for twenty-six years. She didn't want to move. So she pretended not to notice the things that people said to her, the advice they gave.

Not until Gabriella came to see her. Signora welcomed her. Then there was a long silence.

'Will you go back soon to your country?' Gabriella asked at last.

'There is nobody for me to go back to,' Signora said.

'But there is nobody for you here, not now,' Gabriella said.

'Do you want me to leave, Signora Gabriella?'

'Mario always said you would go if he died − you would not stay here against the tradition of the place.'

Signora was shocked. Mario had told her how important tradition was to him and his family. She felt that he was speaking to her from the dead.

She spoke very slowly. 'I think at the end of the month, Signora Gabriella. That is when I will go back to Ireland.'

The other woman looked at her gratefully. She took Signora's hands in hers. 'I am sure you will be much happier,' she said.

'Yes, yes,' Signora said slowly.

◆

Signora had made no plans. She had told no one that she was coming back to Ireland, not even her family. She had very little money, but she had always looked after herself. She would find a room. Then she would decide what to do next.

She was surprised at how much Dublin had changed. There were so many young people − tall, confident, laughing, brightly dressed. Before she left, Dublin had been a grey and dull place. Now it was a whole new world.

She found a place to have a coffee, and a girl of about eighteen served her. The girl had long red hair, like her own hair many years ago. She thought Signora was foreign.

'What country are you from?' she asked in slow English.

'Sicily, in Italy,' Signora said.

'I'm not going there until I can speak the language. I want to know what the men are saying about me.'

'I didn't speak any Italian when I went there,' Signora said, 'but you know, it was all right. No, it was more than all right. I loved it. I stayed for twenty-six years.'

'And when did you come back?'

'Today. Is that your name there on your shirt? Suzi?' she asked quickly, as the girl began to move away.

'Yes, like Suzi Quatro, the singer, you know?'

'Well, Suzi, where could I rent a room, do you think? Somewhere not too expensive,' Signora said.

Suzi thought for a minute. She seemed to be trying to decide something. 'What's your name?' she asked.

'I know this sounds funny, but my name is Signora. It's what they called me in Italy, and I like it.'

'Listen. I don't live at home now, because I don't like living with my family. And only a few weeks ago they were talking about renting my room to someone. It's empty and they'd be pleased to get a few pounds for it.'

'Do you think I could?' Signora's eyes were shining.

'But it's a very ordinary house. They have the television on all the time. They have to shout above the noise and of course my brother's there. Jerry's fourteen and terrible.'

'I just need a place to stay. I'm sure it would be fine.'

Suzi wrote down the address and told her which bus to take. 'Our name's Sullivan. They'll like you because you're a bit older. But don't say you came from me.'

◆

Signora stood outside the Sullivans' house and knocked on the door. Would this be her new home?

Jerry opened the door. He had red hair and he had a sandwich in his hand. 'Yes?' he said.

'Could I speak to your mother or father, please?'

'What about?'

'I want to ask if I can rent a room,' Signora began. At that moment, the boy's father and mother came to the door. Signora repeated her question.

'And why are you looking for a room in this area?' the woman asked.

'I have been away from Ireland for a long time. I don't know many places now but I do need somewhere to live. I had no idea that things had become so expensive and . . . well . . . I came this way because you can see the mountains from here.' For some reason this seemed to please them. 'I would be no trouble. I would sit in my room,' Signora added.

'You haven't even seen the room,' the woman said.

Together they all walked upstairs. It was a small room with an empty cupboard, empty bookshelves and no pictures on the walls. There was no sign of the years that the beautiful Suzi had spent here.

Outside the window it was getting dark. The room looked out over land where there would soon be more houses, but at the moment there was nothing between her and the mountains.

'It's good to have a beautiful view like this,' Signora said. 'I have been living in Italy, and they would call this Vista del Monte, mountain view.'

'That's the name of the school our son goes to, Mountainview,' said the big man.

Signora smiled at him. 'If you'll have me, Mrs Sullivan, Mr Sullivan, . . . I think I've come to a very nice place.'

They sat downstairs and talked, and immediately her gentleness seemed to improve their behaviour. The man cleared the food away from the table. The woman put out her cigarette and turned off the television. The boy sat in the corner watching with interest.

She told them she had lived long years in Italy and that her Italian husband had died there recently. She had come home to Ireland to make her life here.

'And have you no family here?'

'I do have some relatives,' said Signora. 'I will visit them one day.'

They told her that life was hard, that Jimmy worked as a driver and Peggy worked in a supermarket. And then the conversation came back to the room upstairs. She asked if they would like a month's rent now. 'Perhaps I could step outside while you talk about it,' she said, and went out to the back garden.

The Sullivans soon came to the door, their decision made.

'Come for a week, and if you like us and we like you, it could be for a bit longer,' Peggy said.

Signora's eyes shone. '*Grazie, grazie,*'★ she said, before she could stop herself.

◆

The next day, Signora started to look for a job. She asked in restaurants for kitchen work and was politely refused everywhere. She tried a supermarket and a newspaper shop but again without luck. Her search brought her towards the coffee shop where Suzi worked. She went in and the girl looked up, pleased.

'You actually went there! My mum told me someone was renting my room.'

'It's very nice. I wanted to thank you. Tell me, Suzi, why can't I get a job? Just an ordinary job, cleaning, tidying, anything. Am I too old?'

Suzi thought for a minute. 'I think you look a bit too good for

★ *grazie*: the Italian word for *thank you*.

the jobs you're looking for. Perhaps you should aim for something a bit better?'

So Signora decided to show some of her sewing, some pieces of work that she had done in Italy, to fashion shops and designers. Everyone admired her work and soon she was paid to make some baby dresses.

Then, sometimes, when she was sewing in the evenings, Jerry came and knocked on her door.

'Are you busy, Mrs Signora?'

'No, come in, Jerry. It's nice to have company.'

'You can come downstairs, you know.'

'Why don't you bring your school work up here, Jerry? Then you can be company for me and I can help you if you need it.'

They sat together all through the month of May, talking easily. Signora showed great interest in Jerry's school work.

'Read me that poem again. Let's see, what does it mean?'

'It's only an old poem, Mrs Signora.'

'I know, but it must mean something. Let's think.'

So Jerry Sullivan learnt his poems, wrote his stories, did his sums. And a teacher said that Jerry's school work had improved greatly, Suzi reported to Signora. 'My parents should be paying you,' she said.

But History was the only subject that Jerry was really interested in. Jerry thought the teacher, Mr O'Brien, was great.

'He's going to be the Principal of Mountainview, you know, next year,' Jerry explained.

◆

'Your mother's asking you and me to tea on Thursday with Jerry's teacher,' Signora told Suzi.

'Oh, I've heard a story or two about Tony O'Brien,' Suzi said. 'He likes the company of ladies. Be careful, Signora!'

'I'm never going to be interested in a man again,' Signora said honestly.

'I've said that before now, but the interest came back.'

The conversation at the tea party was a little difficult at first. So Signora began to talk, gently, almost dreamily, about all the changes in Ireland she noticed, most of them good ones.

And after that everyone relaxed. They talked like a normal family; more polite than many Tony O'Brien had visited. He had always thought that there was not much hope for Jerry Sullivan. But this strange woman seemed to have had a good effect on the family and the boy.

'I expect you loved Italy, if you stayed there so long.'

'I did, very, very much.'

'I've never been there myself, but there's another teacher at our school who lives, sleeps and breathes Italy. His name's Aidan Dunne. You really should meet him.'

♦

Signora decided that she must try to get a teaching job of some sort. She could teach Italian to beginners, couldn't she? Perhaps this man at Jerry's school, the one that was a lover of Italy, might know some group or organization that needed Italian lessons. What was his name? Mr Aidan Dunne, that was it. She could ask him.

She took a bus to the school and knocked on the door of the teachers' room. A man came to answer it. He had thin brown hair and anxious eyes.

'Mr Dunne? I've come to talk to you about Italian.'

'Do you know, I *knew* that one day someone would knock at the door and say that to me.'

They both smiled and it was clear that they were going to be friends.

Aidan Dunne explained about the evening class that he wanted so much. But the Department of Education was not being very helpful about money for the class. He had been worried that they might not be able to afford a good teacher. Now he felt there was some hope again.

It had been a long time since Signora had been admired. She liked it.

Signora told him how she had lived so long in Sicily and that she could teach not only the language, but perhaps something about the life too. Could there be a class on Italian artists, for example? And then there could be Italian music and wines and food.

He was admiring her openly now. It had been a long time since Signora had been admired. She liked it. And she liked this good man, trying to share his own love of another country with the people around here.

The school bell rang. 'We can talk more at four o'clock, if it's convenient for you,' Aidan said.

'I have nothing else to do,' she replied.

'Would you like to sit in our library?' he asked.

'Very much.'

She sat there reading through the books they had on Italy. Aidan Dunne had probably bought them with his own money. Then she thought of Dublin. Where would they find the people to attend the class? She and Mr Dunne. She and Aidan. She shook herself a little. She mustn't start dreaming. That had been her problem, people had said.

At that moment the door opened and Aidan stood there. He was smiling all over his face.

Chapter 3 Bill

It was such a pity, Bill Burke often felt, that he was not in love with Grania Dunne. She worked in the bank with him and was about twenty-three, his own age. She came from a normal kind of home. She was attractive and easy to talk to.

They often discussed the people they loved. Grania told Bill about this man that she just couldn't get out of her mind. He was as old as her father and smoked, but she had never met anyone who attracted her so much.

Bill understood, because he loved Lizzie Duffy, the most unsuitable person in the world. Lizzie was beautiful but she was also trouble. She said that she loved Bill, or she thought she did; but she had never met anyone so serious in her whole life. Most of Lizzie's other friends were only interested in having fun. Like Lizzie, they had little interest in getting or keeping jobs. It was stupid loving Lizzie.

Bill knew that Lizzie had borrowed a lot of money from his bank. And she never seemed to pay it back. 'You'll have to do well in banking,' she often said to Bill. 'I can only marry a successful man. When we're twenty-five and get married, you must be on your way to the top.' As she spoke, she gave her beautiful laugh, showing all her small white teeth, and she shook her long golden hair. But Bill knew that she meant it.

'Lizzie, don't,' he had to say as she ordered another bottle of wine. He would have to pay for it, and she was talking about wanting a holiday too.

It was becoming very difficult for Bill. He lived with his parents and his sister, Olive. Olive was twenty-five but she had the mind of an eight-year-old child. She was not ill but she would never be normal and would need to be looked after. Bill earned a lot more than his father, who had worked hard to give him a good start in life, so he had hoped to help his family financially. And he really needed a new suit too. Where could he find all this money? It was, of course, possible to borrow it. Possible but not desirable.

That evening, there was a talk at the bank on job opportunities. The speaker said that there would be opportunities to work abroad in a year's time. The world was open to young people who could speak other languages and who had special skills. If they were interested, they should start to prepare themselves now.

Bill started thinking. If he was chosen to work in a European capital, he would earn good money. Lizzie might come and live with him in Paris or Rome or Madrid.

He started to look at information about language courses. They were very expensive and he didn't know how to choose. As usual, he talked to his friend Grania about it.

'My father's starting an evening class in Italian at his school,' she said. 'It begins in September and they're looking for pupils.'

'Would it be good?'

'I don't know.' Grania was always so honest. 'But they've got an Italian teacher, called Signora. My father says she's great.'

Bill told his parents that night that he was going to learn Italian. His father said it was good to see a boy improving himself all the time.

He told Lizzie about the class. 'Would you like to learn too?' he asked hopefully.

'What for?' Lizzie laughed, and he laughed too, although he didn't know why.

'Well, so that you could speak a bit of Italian if we went there, you know.'

'But don't Italians speak English?'

'Some of them do, but I'm still going to learn it. The lessons are on Tuesdays and Thursdays.'

'I would come with you Bill, but honestly I just don't have the money.' Her eyes were so big.

'I'll pay for your course,' Bill said. Now he would definitely have to borrow some money from a bank.

They were nice to him in the bank.

'You can borrow more than that,' a helpful young man said.

'I know, but it might be difficult to pay it back,' said Bill. Then he thought of the suit and he thought of his parents. He'd love to take them out somewhere special. He borrowed twice as much money as he had intended to.

◆

21

Grania told Bill how pleased her father was that she had got two new members for the class.

'I'm going to try my friend Fiona tonight,' Grania said.

'Fiona who works in the hospital?' Bill had a feeling that Grania was trying to get him and Fiona together.

'Yeah, you know about Fiona. A great friend of mine. I tell her all my problems; like when I discovered about Tony taking my father's job. Did I tell you about that?'

She had told him many times.

'If you went back to Tony,' he said, 'would your father be very upset about it?'

Grania looked at Bill quickly. How did he know exactly what was in her own mind? 'I've decided that I'll wait a bit,' she said slowly, 'until things are better in my Dad's life. Then he might be able to face something like that.'

◆

Lizzie had become excited about the lessons. 'I'm telling everyone that we'll be speaking Italian soon,' she laughed happily, the night before they began. 'What should I wear?'

Only Lizzie would want to know that. Other people might ask if they should bring a notebook or a dictionary.

'Something that won't attract too much attention,' Bill suggested hopefully. It was a silly suggestion. Lizzie didn't have clothes that wouldn't attract attention.

'But what exactly?'

Bill knew that he had to choose a colour. 'I love the red,' he said.

Her eyes shone. It was easy to please Lizzie. 'I'll try it on now,' she said, and got out her short red skirt and red and white shirt. She looked beautiful, fresh and young, just like a magazine picture with her golden hair.

◆

The evening classes were held in a school in a poor area of the city. The building was dusty and dirty and it needed painting.

22

But Bill was pleasantly surprised when they went in. Big pictures covered the walls, pictures of Rome and of Italian art, of Italian wine and food. There was also a table in the room, covered in red, white and green paper. On the table were paper plates that seemed to have real food on them ... little pieces of meat and cheese. Someone had made a very big effort.

Bill hoped that it would all go well: for the strange woman with the red and grey hair called Signora, for the kind man standing at the back who must be Grania's father, for all the people who sat nervously waiting for it to start.

When they were all quiet, Signora introduced herself. '*Mi chiamo Signora. Come si chiama?*' she asked the man who must be Grania's father.

'*Mi chiamo Aidan,*' he said. And they continued like this around the classroom.

Lizzie loved it. '*Mi chiamo Lizzie,*' she cried, and everyone smiled admiringly.

'Let's try to make our names more Italian. You could say: "*Mi chiamo Elizabetta*".'

Lizzie loved that even more and repeated it several times.

Then they all wrote *Mi chiamo* and their names on big pieces of paper and fixed them on their clothes. And they learned to say how they were, what time it was, what day and date it was and where they lived.

'*Chi è?*' Signora asked, pointing at Bill.

'*Guglielmo,*' the class all shouted back.

Soon they knew everyone's names in Italian and the class had clearly relaxed.

'*Bene,*' said Signora. 'Now we have ten minutes more.' Everyone was surprised. Had two hours passed already? 'You have all worked so hard that we can have something to eat now. But first you must pronounce the words for the food.'

Like children, the thirty adults ate the meat and cheese and pronounced the words.

When it ended, Bill and Lizzie walked to the bus stop.

'*Ti amo*,' she said to him suddenly.

'What's that?' he asked.

'It means I love you!' Lizzie said, smiling.

'How do you know?' He was so surprised.

'I asked her before we left. She said they were the two most beautiful words in the world.'

'They are, they are,' said Bill.

♦

Aidan Dunne watched the success of the evening class with a pleasure that surprised him. Week after week they came to the school, on bicycles, motorcycles, buses, even that well-dressed woman in the BMW. What was she doing here? And there was the beautiful girl with the golden hair and her nice boyfriend in his good suit. And the dark, violent-looking Luigi, and the older man called Lorenzo. What a surprising variety.

But the people in the class seemed to be forming a special sort of relationship. They were like children, wanting to do well. Possibly because Signora believed they could all do anything, they began to believe it too. For Signora, it was only possible to feel love for the Italian language. And that is what they felt.

Signora had asked Aidan if he would like her to make a cover for the chair in his study at home.

'Come and see the room,' Aidan suggested suddenly. 'Are you free on Saturday morning?'

'I can be free any time,' she said.

She brought materials for the chair. 'I thought that yellow would be right, from what you told me,' she said, holding up a rich golden colour. 'Do you want to show it to your wife before I begin?'

'No, no. I mean this is my room, really.'

'Yes, of course.' Signora never asked any questions.

Aidan hadn't told Nell or his daughters about the visit, and he was glad that they weren't there that morning. Together he and Signora drank to the success of the Italian class.

◆

Bill was taking sandwiches to work. He could certainly not afford to eat in the bank's restaurant. He was worried about how he was going to pay his debts next month.

Lizzie had already told Bill that she would have to miss the next Italian class. Her mother was coming to Dublin and she wanted to meet her at the station. 'And Bill, could you lend me the money for a taxi? My mother hates buses.'

Bill gave her the money and kissed her. 'Will I meet your mother this time?'

'I hope so, Bill. But she knows so many people, you see. They take all her time.'

Bill thought it was strange that none of these friends were able to meet her with a car or taxi. But he didn't say it. He knew that Lizzie's mother lived in the west of Ireland and belonged to a group of artists and painters. He had the idea that she mixed with rich and important people.

So he was surprised when Lizzie telephoned him after his class. She sounded upset.

'What's wrong, Lizzie?'

'Everything,' she said. 'Could you come round here, Bill? I need you.'

It seemed that her mother had only wanted to meet her for a quick drink at the station. It was always the same; she never had any time for Lizzie.

'I had her supper ready. But she said she was meeting an artist friend of hers. She said she'd only met me to keep me quiet. She actually pushed past me.' And then Lizzie told Bill for the first time how her mother had left her father, herself and her sisters when they were still quite young.

Bill was sad and angry that this woman had upset Lizzie. Why couldn't she be nice for a few hours?

'How did your mother live when she left your father?' Bill wanted to know. 'Did she have a job?'

Lizzie looked a bit embarrassed. 'I didn't know this until recently, Bill. But when she left us, she did cleaning and housework in a big house.'

Bill couldn't believe what he heard. So this was the free and artistic life that he had always felt rather jealous of. It had seemed so different to his own dull family life.

'It's all right,' he said gently to Lizzie. 'No families are perfect. Perhaps when the weather is better we could take the bus and visit your mother. It's never too late to change.'

On the way home Bill felt more hopeful than he had felt for a long time. He didn't need to think that he might be too boring for Lizzie. He knew now that she wanted to feel safe, to be loved and have a home, and he could give her all those things. Of course she would still want to spend too much money. But her mother had worked, so perhaps he could lead Lizzie towards regular work too.

Bill Burke walked on through the night as other people drove by in taxis or cars. But it didn't matter. He was a lucky man.

Chapter 4   Lou

When Lou was fifteen, three men with sticks had come into his parents' shop. They were taking the cigarettes and money when they heard a police car. Lou had shown them how to escape, over the back wall. His father had been very angry.

'You let them get away!' he shouted at Lou.

'It's best like this, Dad. They won't come back and break our windows. They'll be grateful to us,' Lou replied.

His mother had understood. 'We don't want to attract trouble,' she had said.

In fact, six weeks later a man came into the shop to buy cigarettes. Lou was serving. Robin introduced himself, asked Lou's name and then said: 'Here's a leg of lamb for your mother, Lou. You're a good boy – you'll hear from us.'

His mother had cooked the lamb and asked no questions.

Lou had felt excited at the thought of being so close to the criminal world. He was glad when he met Robin again, by chance it seemed. He did his first real job for the thieves then. He was told to get work cleaning in a cinema. He had to leave a door unlocked at night. The thieves got in and took all the money. They gave him one hundred pounds.

Lou never asked Robin for a job. By the time he was nineteen, he had only helped him twice. Lou was working in an electrical shop. But he wanted to meet Robin again, and it happened, unexpectedly, at a nightclub.

'You're looking well, Lou. Working at the moment?'

'Nothing that can't be changed, if necessary.'

'Busy place here, isn't it?' Robin said, looking at the notes that were passing across the bar.

And that was the job. The thieves wanted to rob the van that left the club with all the money every night. They wanted someone to stop the van for about five minutes by driving their car in front of it. Someone that the club knew well, who came there regularly. They bought Lou a car.

♦

Six weeks later, Lou met Robin again.

'Been going to that nightclub regularly?' Robin asked.

'Twice, three times a week. They know me well now.'

'Don't drink tonight. And perhaps I'll show you a good place to park the car.'

'That would be great.' Lou asked no other details.

At about ten o'clock that night, he parked the car where Robin had shown him. Then he went into the club. Almost immediately he met the first girl that he ever thought he could love and live with for the rest of his life. Her name was Suzi and she was tall and beautiful with long red hair.

They danced and they talked for four and a half hours. They liked the same kind of films and music. They both liked Indian food. They both hoped to go to America one day. He knew it would be normal to drive her home. But he couldn't. He had a job to do.

'Can I see you again tomorrow, Suzi?'

'So has tonight ended?' Suzi asked.

'I've got to meet someone here a bit later. But tomorrow we'll go anywhere you want, I promise.'

'Really?' she said, upset and annoyed. 'Goodnight Lou.' And she picked up her coat and walked out into the night.

The robbery worked perfectly. At the right minute Lou drove his car backwards in front of the van with the money. Then the car stopped. He pretended that he couldn't start it again. While he was trying, dark figures escaped with the money over a wall.

Nobody thought that Lou had had a part in what happened. The people who worked in the club told police that they knew him; he was a very nice man. He got a good report from the electrical shop.

Lou heard later that the thieves had been carrying guns. He felt a bit sick then. He had thought that they still carried sticks. But when he next saw Robin, the man gave Lou a thousand pounds.

◆

While he was trying, dark figures escaped with the money over a wall.

The day after the robbery, Lou went to Suzi's café at lunchtime with a red rose. They met most nights after that. Lou was able to buy Suzi nice things, but it seemed to worry her when he pulled out twenty pound notes.

'Hey, Lou, where do you get money like that?'

'I work, don't I?'

'Yes, and I know what they pay you. You're not doing anything that you shouldn't do, are you, Lou?'

'Not at the moment, no,' he said.

Suzi had the sense to say nothing more. And for the first time, Lou hoped that he wouldn't meet Robin again.

◆

As usual though, Robin found Lou when he wanted him. Robin already knew about Suzi. He expected that Lou would want to buy a house soon. Robin could, of course, help him with that, but there was a job to do first. They needed a place to store five or six boxes every week. A place where there was a lot of activity, so people could go in and out unnoticed with these boxes.

'I'll think,' said Lou. 'But, well, actually, Robin, I'm thinking that . . . I don't want to be part of this in future.'

The look on Robin's face was terrible to see. 'When you're part of this, you're always part of it. That's the way it is.'

'I see,' said Lou.

◆

That night Suzi said she wasn't free. She had promised to help the Italian woman who rented a room in her parents' house. They were going to tidy some rooms in Mountainview school, ready for an evening class. Lou said he would help too, and he was glad that he did help. Because there was a storeroom with boxes in it in the part of the school where the classes would be. Empty boxes.

'Shall we throw these out?' Suzi suggested.

Slowly Lou spoke. 'Why don't I just put them in a corner? You never know when you might need them.'

'You're right,' Signora said. 'We might use them for a table in an Italian restaurant, or a car in the garage.'

'Good woman, Signora,' Lou said.

♦

'I found somewhere,' said Lou when Robin telephoned him at work.

'I knew you would, Lou.'

Lou told him where it was and about the activity every Tuesday and Thursday, with thirty people.

'And have you joined the class?' said Robin.

'No. I have trouble speaking English. Why would I want to learn Italian?'

'I think you should, Lou.'

When he got home that night, there was an envelope waiting for him. It contained five hundred pounds.

♦

Suzi found it hard to understand why Lou suddenly wanted to learn Italian. He told her that he wanted to improve himself.

He went to the first lesson like a man walking to his death. But it was surprisingly enjoyable. '*Mi chiamo Luigi*,' he told the others. They were such a strange group of people. Perhaps they wouldn't question why he was there.

After two weeks he heard from Robin. Some boxes were going to come in on Tuesday, at the time when people were arriving for the class. Lou didn't know the van driver. The four boxes were in in a minute, then the man was gone. On Thursday they were taken out again.

Lou made himself popular with Signora by helping with the boxes. Sometimes they covered them with paper and put knives and forks on them.

'*Quanto costa il piatto del giorno*?' Signora asked. And they repeated it again and again until they could ask for anything. Perhaps it was childish but Lou liked it. He even thought that he and Suzi might go to Italy one day.

And so it continued. Weeks of boxes, in on Tuesday and out on Thursday. Lou didn't want to think about what was in them. He knew it must be drugs.

◆

One of the nice things about working in a café was listening to people's conversations. Suzi said she could write a book from the bits of conversation she heard.

One day an older man came in with an attractive girl. She was wearing a bank uniform. They didn't look very relaxed together, Suzi thought.

'I'm only agreeing to meet you because I want a good cup of coffee,' she said.

'But please, Grania, can't we talk?'

'We *are* talking, Tony.'

'I think I love you,' he said. 'Let's go out for dinner and talk like we used to talk.'

Suzi cleared the next table very slowly. He was a nice old man. The girl should give him a chance.

'Just dinner then,' Grania said, and they held hands.

◆

Suzi and Lou decided that they would marry next year.

'I'll never like anyone more,' Suzi told Signora.

Signora admired Suzi's ring. 'It's very, very beautiful,' she said.

'It's only glass, Signora, but it looks real, doesn't it?'

Signora, who had always loved jewellery, but never had any, knew that the stone was real. And very expensive. She began to worry about Luigi. How had he managed to buy this? Of course, Robin had arranged it. Lou had only had to pay £250, but

32

another £9,500 had already been paid towards a ring before he and Suzi went into the shop.

◆

It was the Christmas party in the Italian class. They weren't going to meet again for two weeks. There were flags with *Buon Natale*★ written on them. They wore paper hats and had a few glasses of wine.

In the middle of all this, Luigi suddenly had a terrible thought. Where would they store the boxes for the next two weeks? The school would be locked. Why hadn't he thought of this before? He knew he had to act quickly.

'How are you getting home?' he asked Signora, when they had finished clearing the tables. 'Is Mr Dunne meeting you?'

'Yes, he did say he might.' Her face went a little pink. She felt worried. If Luigi thought there was something between her and Aidan Dunne, then the whole class must think so. She didn't want people to start talking about them. Aidan Dunne only thought of her as a friend. That was all.

'Why don't you leave now, then?' Luigi said. 'It's late. I'll lock the doors for you.'

'*Grazie, Luigi.*' She gave him the key. Now he might still be able to get the boxes in and out.

◆

The evening before Christmas they worked long hours in the electrical shop. Just before closing time, Robin came in.

'Happy Christmas, Lou. I came to tell you that you can stop learning Italian, if you want. We've found another place for the boxes.'

'What?'

'Yeah, the last van driver made a silly mistake. We don't want to be seen around the school now.'

★*Buon Natale*: an Italian phrase that means *Happy Christmas*.

'What will happen to the driver?' Lou asked, afraid.

'He'll never work for us again.'

So that was what you had to do to get out of this, Lou thought. Just do one job badly and you were never called again. It was so simple.

'I've bought a present for you, Lou. It's a television for you and Suzi.'

'I can't take it,' Lou said. 'She'd know it was stolen.'

'It's not stolen. I've paid for it,' said Robin.

It was, of course, the most expensive television in the whole shop. Suzi would never accept it. But Lou had an idea. He still had Signora's school key. He put the television in the back of his car. It was midnight when he drove up to the school. With difficulty he carried the big television into the classroom. He had written a note which he left on it: *Buon Natale a Lei, Signora, e a tutti.*

The school would have a television. There was nothing on it to show where it had come from. They would never know.

And when Robin asked Lou to do another job, the job would be done badly. Lou would be told that he could never work again. He could continue with his life.

◆

It was Christmas Day. Lou went round to Suzi's parents' house for tea and Christmas cake. Signora was there.

'Signora!' he said.

'Luigi.' She seemed pleased to see him.

They talked about the presents they had received. In the middle of the conversation, Lou remembered that he still had Signora's school key. She put it in her bag and the conversation continued. No one noticed him giving it to her.

◆

The class began again on the first Tuesday in January. They were all there. Nobody was missing from the thirty who had joined in September.

34

The Principal, Tony O'Brien, was there too, and Mr Dunne. They were smiling all over their faces. The class had been given a present . . . a television. Who had done it? Was it one of the class?

The Principal was pleased but he said that if nobody knew the answer they would have to change the locks on the doors. Because somebody must have a key.

And suddenly Signora looked up and looked at Luigi.

Lou tried to leave quickly when the class was over.

'Not helping me with the boxes tonight, Luigi?' Signora asked.

'Sorry, Signora, I forgot.'

Together they lifted the empty boxes into the store cupboard.

'Luigi, you are going to marry Suzi, the daughter of the house where I stay,' Signora said. 'I want to discuss that with you, and the ring.'

'Yes, it's beautiful, isn't it. But it's only glass.'

'No, I know it's real. It cost thousands, Luigi. And that television cost hundreds.'

'What are you saying?'

'I don't know. What are *you* saying to *me*?'

He felt ashamed. No one had made him ashamed like this before. 'I'm saying . . .' he began. 'I'm saying it's finished. There won't be any more of it.'

'And are these things stolen, the ring and the television?'

'No, they were paid for by people I worked for.'

'But you don't work for them now?'

'No, I don't. I promise.' He wanted her to believe him.

'So Suzi won't ever need to know anything about this?'

'No, Signora. I'll be good. I promise.'

'Good luck, Luigi,' said Signora, and locked the door behind them.

Chapter 5   Connie

The wedding of Connie O'Connor and Harry Kane was going to be in the Hayes Hotel. Miss O'Connor had been the receptionist at the hotel since it opened two years before. She was excellent at her job: beautiful, a good organizer, polite with customers, always in control. She had met Mr Kane at the hotel. He was the most attractive man she had ever seen, tall with thick brown hair and an easy smile. He came to the hotel every Wednesday for meetings and to entertain people to lunch.

Connie had slowly learnt more and more about Harry Kane. He was almost thirty and lived alone. His name was sometimes seen in the newspapers, with the names of other rich and famous people. He, with two older partners, had a new and very successful insurance business. Some people said that the business was growing too fast, that there would be trouble. But it showed no signs of it.

♦

Connie's mother slept in the same hotel room as Connie the night before the wedding.

'You *are* happy?' her mother asked her suddenly.

'Oh, mother, of course I'm happy,' Connie said. 'I'm just afraid that I might not be good enough for him, you know. He's a very successful man.'

'You've been good enough for him until now,' her mother said. 'Now, make sure he gives you money for yourself. Invest it. Then, if something goes wrong, you'll be all right.'

'Oh, Mother.' Connie felt sad. Her mother was speaking from her own experience. Connie's father, a dentist, had died when she was nineteen. He had left debts that none of them had known about. They had lost the family home. None of the children was able to go to university as they had planned. Connie's mother never forgave her husband.

♦

It was the best wedding that Dublin had seen for years. Afterwards they spent two weeks in the Bahamas. Connie had thought that those two weeks would be the best of her life. And she did enjoy some of it. She liked talking to Harry and laughing with him. But when he touched her, something changed. She could not relax. She could not understand her own coldness. Perhaps she was afraid of men after the unhappiness her own father had caused. Harry could not understand either. He was upset and angry and, almost before it had really started, their relationship was in trouble.

♦

A few months after their wedding Connie found that she was expecting a baby. This gave them both new hope.

'You've made me the happiest man in the world,' he said. 'I'll do anything for you.'

Connie had stopped working at the hotel, but she kept busy and tried to share in Harry's life as much as possible. She often drove to see Harry's parents. And she gave dinners for Harry's partners and their wives. The wives were almost twenty years older than her. They hadn't liked her much in the beginning, but now they told their husbands that she was the perfect wife for Harry Kane. It was a good thing that he hadn't married his secretary, that unpleasant Siobhan Casey.

Connie didn't know that before she was married there had been a relationship between Harry and Siobhan Casey. She was very shocked when she realized that he was meeting her now. He hadn't tried to make a success of their life together. She'd been married seven months and was expecting a child. No man had a more comfortable lifestyle. She kept their big new house beautifully. But he wanted something more than she could give.

The months passed and they communicated less and less. A short time after their son, Richard, was born, a lawyer asked Harry to come to a meeting in his office. The lawyer had been a friend of Connie's father. He explained to Harry that Mrs Kane had asked him to prepare a legal document, dividing their property between them.

'But she knows that half of mine is hers.' Harry was more shocked than he had ever been in his life.

'Yes, but there are other things to think about,' the lawyer said. 'You must agree that your company grew very quickly. Financially, it may not be as safe as it seems. You know that your wife's father's investments were not enough to look after her family when ...'

'That was totally different.'

'And we understand that Mrs Kane is expecting a second child, and that she had a successful career before she married you.'

'That was only a receptionist's job. She can have anything she wants now. What's she complaining about?'

'Mrs Kane is not complaining,' said Murphy. 'She is only afraid that something might happen to your company. Then you would be left without the things you have worked so hard for.'

'And what does she suggest?'

Connie's lawyer wanted almost everything put legally in her name; their house and a large amount of what Harry earned from the company. She would form another company with its own directors.

'And if I refuse?'

'I'm sure you don't want the newspapers and the public to hear about this. It would be bad for business ...'

Harry Kane signed the document.

He drove straight back to his house and walked into the sunny kitchen where Connie sat feeding baby Richard. He stood and looked at his beautiful wife and son. Soon they would have another child. In a way she was right to protect herself.

'I saw your lawyer,' he said.

For months she hadn't come near him or shown any feeling

for him. But now she put her arms around his neck. 'Harry, don't be angry, please. We have such a nice life.'

'You didn't ask me if I signed.'

She pulled away. 'I know you did. Because it's right and because it might help you, too, in the end.'

'Why didn't you tell me what you were doing, Connie?'

'I was lonely and frightened. I didn't want my children to have the same experience as I did. And I didn't want to hate you like my mother hated my father.'

'I see.'

'Can't you be my friend, Harry? I love you and want the best for you even if I can't always show it.'

'I don't know,' he said. 'I don't know.'

◆

The new baby was a girl, called Veronica. And there were two more babies after that. To other people, the Kanes seemed to be very happy. But Harry Kane was seen with other women, and his secretary still followed him around.

The years passed and the children grew up fast. The oldest boy had nearly finished at school. Veronica was hoping to study medicine. The other boys were full of life.

Harry seemed to work hard, and he never had time for a family holiday. He had to go abroad a lot too. Work, he said.

Of course Connie wasn't happy. Some of her friends thought she should leave Harry. So why did she stay? Because it was better for the family. Because it was too much effort to change everything. Because this wasn't a bad life. Harry was pleasant when he was there.

And then one day Harry Kane came home and told his family that his company was closing the next day. People's investments had been lost – the money they had saved all their lives.

It would be all over the newspapers. There would be newspaper reporters and photographers at the door. What had caused it? Perhaps they hadn't been quite as careful as other companies had. They hadn't always asked enough questions, checked everything fully.

'Your mother always told me that this could happen,' Harry said to his children. 'And I didn't listen.'

'Oh, Dad, it doesn't matter,' Veronica said.

'It could happen to anyone,' Richard said bravely.

Connie saw Harry's eyes fill with tears. She realized it was time to speak.

She told the children that they would stay with her mother in the country until she and their father had arranged everything. And no, she said, they wouldn't have to sell the house. Yes, they could still go to university. There would be enough money for that and also to pay back the money that their investors had lost. Their father was a very clever businessman. They had their house, and a lot of money in another company, of which she was the director.

The children left in a taxi later that evening.

'What am I going to do, Connie?' Harry said.

'I'll keep as much of my money as I need for the children. I'll put the rest back into your company to pay back the people who lost everything.'

'God, why do you always have to be so perfect?' said Harry. 'You took the money. Keep it. Those investors knew what they were doing. It's their problem.'

Connie's face went white with anger. This man cared about no one except himself. She stood up and walked to the door.

'Go on, leave,' he shouted. 'Go and tell all your friends.'

She hadn't intended to, but she turned and hit him across the face. Then she closed the door behind her.

♦

The next day was like a terrible dream. Some of it was spent in the lawyer's office, where her financial position was explained to

She turned and hit him across the face.

her. Her money had been well invested. She was a very rich woman. She could see what they thought of her husband. They didn't even try to hide it.

Then she and Harry went to the bank. Their bankers were very surprised to see this money appearing from nowhere. By midday they had an agreement. The bank would arrange a plan to rescue the investors.

After that, Harry and his partners had to speak to newspaper reporters. They said that money had been kept specifically for a situation like this.

'Of course, we will look after the people who have invested with us,' Harry said straight to the camera.

And Connie, watching on television, felt a little sick.

◆

And so time passed. Things were almost normal again. The children were becoming independent, two in work, two at university.

But people who knew the facts felt that Harry wasn't grateful enough to Connie. He was seen in public with Siobhan Casey, who was now a director of his company. And so Connie's lawyers prepared another document. It was similar to the first, and again gave her a share of the money that Harry's company made. The papers were sent to Harry's office. His face was hard the day he signed them. She knew he would try to punish her for it.

'I'll be away for a few days,' he said that evening. 'I'm combining business with a holiday in the Bahamas.'

She didn't try to stop him. He went out later, shutting the door loudly behind him. This was no way to live a life.

◆

Connie began to think that she might have a holiday herself. It was years since she had been away anywhere. And she had always wanted to go to Italy. So when she read in the newspaper that there was a new evening class in Italian up at Mountainview school, she decided to join.

She enjoyed it. This very special woman, Signora, not much older than herself, was a natural teacher. She spoke quietly, but she had everyone's attention. She never criticized, but she expected people to learn what they were taught.

And Connie liked the other people in the class – Guglielmo and Elizabetta, Luigi, Lorenzo and the others. Slowly they were all becoming more confident and hopeful about their dream of a class holiday in Italy next summer. Connie – Constanza – would definitely like to go.

When it rained, she sometimes drove people home, especially Lorenzo. He was a big, simple man of about sixty, who lived and worked in his family's hotel. Everyone else went home to relax or went out. But Lorenzo, whose real name was Laddy, went back to work.

Sometimes he talked of his sister's son, Gus, who owned the hotel. Gus worked so hard. And now there was a possibility that he might lose his hotel. There had been a problem some time ago with an insurance and investment company. But at the last moment it had been all right and they had got their money.

As Connie listened, she knew that it was Harry's company, and that these were the people that Harry hadn't cared about. So what was the new problem, she asked.

It seemed that it was all part of the old problem. The company had made them all invest large amounts again. It was to thank the company for looking after them last time. Lorenzo didn't understand it very well but he was worried. The hotel needed building work and decoration. Gus didn't know what to do. Everything he had was in this new investment.

When Connie got to Lorenzo's hotel, she went inside to talk to Gus. Here she heard the full story. Gus had been investing large amounts in two companies abroad for five years now. The directors were Harry Kane and Siobhan Casey. They had told Gus that it was necessary to invest with them, if he wanted them to rescue his hotel business. Connie immediately took out her chequebook and wrote Gus a very large cheque.

'But why are you doing this, Constanza?' Gus asked. 'I can't take this money. I can't. It's too much.'

She pointed at Harry's name on the document. 'That man is my husband. He has lied to you. I can't let him do this to people. See you on Tuesday, Lorenzo,' she said, and she was gone.

◆

As usual, Harry wasn't there when she got home. It was late but she telephoned her lawyer and made an appointment for the next day. It was eleven o'clock at night by the time he had finished talking to her.

'What will you do now?' she asked him.

'Telephone the police,' the lawyer said. 'Your husband is guilty of giving false information to people and of using their money illegally.'

Harry did not come home that night. The next day Connie walked up the steps of her husband's office. Their meeting would end his life as he knew it.

The police were already there.

'You didn't have to tell them, Connie,' Harry said. 'You had everything you needed. Why did you do it?'

'Because it wasn't right, Harry. You were rescued once. Wasn't that enough?'

She saw Siobhan Casey in her office. She was sitting with bankers, lawyers and police.

Connie walked out of the door and got into her car. She didn't look back.

Chapter 6 Laddy

When Signora was choosing Italian names for people, she tried to make sure they began with the same letter. The big simple man was called Laddy. 'Ah, Lorenzo,' she said.

Laddy liked the name. 'Lorenzo. *Mi chiamo Lorenzo.*' he said. He was very pleased.

◆

Laddy had grown up on a farm. Both his parents had died in a train accident when he was eight, and his oldest sister, Rose, had always looked after him. She had hoped that he would one day manage the farm. But Laddy was slow at learning. He was a good boy, he tried hard, but he was slow. By the time he was sixteen, it was clear that Rose would always run the farm.

So Rose married Shay, a strange, silent man who worked on the farm. He did the work and ate and slept on the farm. That was all. It was not a marriage of love. It was simply convenient. They had a son, Gus. Laddy loved little Gus.

Then Shay died suddenly. He fell and hit his head. Some people said that he had always drunk too much. Alone now, Rose made a decision. She would sell the farm and they would go and live in Dublin.

In Dublin, Laddy found work as a porter in a small hotel. There, they soon thought of Laddy as part of the family. He was invited to live in the hotel, and this suited everyone.

Rose became a nurse. She had trained as a nurse before her parents died. She was still an attractive woman in her forties, but she didn't want to marry again. One loveless marriage was enough. And she had Gus and Laddy.

The years passed peacefully enough. Gus did well at school and then studied Hotel Management. He loved his work. He was always prepared to work the longest hours and do the hardest jobs to learn the hotel business.

Laddy was very upset when his employers decided to sell their hotel. He was going to lose his job. At about the same time, Gus met the girl of his dreams. She was called Maggie and was full of life and confidence. She had trained as a cook and was perfect for Gus, in Rose's mind. All Gus and Maggie needed now was a hotel job together. It would be great to buy a small place and to slowly improve it.

'Couldn't you buy my hotel?' Laddy suggested. It was perfect, but of course they couldn't afford it.

'If you give me a room in the hotel to live in, I'll give you the money,' Rose said. It would be a home for Laddy and a start in business for Gus and Maggie.

At first it was not easy to make a success of the hotel. They were paying out more money than they were earning.

'I can work harder,' said Laddy, anxious to help.

'Thank you, Laddy, but there aren't many guests.' Maggie was very kind to her husband's Uncle Laddy.

'Don't worry, Laddy,' said Rose. 'Gus and Maggie will have some ideas. Soon it will be very busy, you'll see.'

And she was right. Gus and Maggie worked at it night and day. The number of regular visitors slowly grew, and these visitors told other people about it.

Gus and Maggie had two children, beautiful little girls. And Rose was one of the happiest women in Ireland.

◆

One day, something happened that gave Laddy a new interest. One of the hotel guests asked where he could play snooker. When Laddy found a snooker hall, the man asked Laddy to have a game with him.

'I'm afraid I don't play, sir,' said Laddy.

'I'll show you,' the man said.

And then it happened. Laddy was naturally good at the game. The man didn't believe he had never played before. He learned the order of the balls: yellow, green, brown, blue, pink, black. He hit them easily and with style. People stood around to watch.

A few months later, he was winning competitions. He had his picture in the paper and he was invited to join a club. He was famous in a small way.

Rose watched all this with great pleasure. Her brother was a person of importance at last. So when she discovered that she was seriously ill, she didn't worry about Laddy's future. She knew that he would always live with Gus and Maggie. He was fine.

◆

'We'll make sure that there's as little pain as possible,' the doctor said.

'Oh, I know you will,' said Rose. 'Now, I'd really like to go into a hospice, where I can be looked after. My family have a hotel to run. I'd prefer not to be there. They would give me too much time.'

When Rose's family came to visit her in the hospice, she didn't tell them about the pain and sickness. She told them all the good things about the place and the work it was doing. The months passed, and she became very thin. But at least her mind was still working well, she said.

In fact it was working too well for Gus and Maggie. They couldn't hide from her the trouble they had.

'You have to tell me what it is,' she said to Gus and Maggie. 'You cannot leave this room without telling me. I'll only imagine that it's even worse than it is.'

They told her the story. They had taken out insurance with a company that had closed. The owner, Harry Kane, had said on television that nobody would lose their investment, the banks would rescue them. But they were still afraid of losing the hotel, their hopes and dreams and future.

Tears poured down Rose's face.

'I knew it was a mistake to tell you,' Gus said.

'No, of course you had to tell me. And please tell me everything that happens after this.'

As the days passed, they brought her letters from the bank. It seemed that the bank were definitely going to rescue the investors. Rose read everything to make sure she had understood it perfectly.

'Does Laddy understand how nearly we lost everything?' she asked.

'He understands at a level of his own,' said Maggie. And Rose realized that Laddy would always be in understanding hands.

She died peacefully.

♦

She never knew that a woman called Siobhan Casey would call at the hotel. Siobhan Casey explained that it was necessary for Gus and Maggie to invest a large amount with Mr Kane's new company. She said that they were lucky, that in similar situations investors had not been rescued. Mr Kane had organized this personally. And now he was being supported by those people whose businesses he had saved.

At first the amount suggested was not large, but then it increased. Gus and Maggie worried about it. But they *had* been rescued; perhaps in business this was normal. Miss Casey had told them that she worked with very powerful people. It might be silly to annoy them.

Gus and Maggie told Laddy nothing. They just tried to spend less money. But Laddy realized something was wrong. The hotel breakfasts were not quite so big. They couldn't afford fresh flowers now.

♦

An Italian businessman, his wife and two sons came to stay in the hotel. The man was busy in offices all day, his wife was busy shopping. Their two sons were bored and so Laddy offered to take them to play snooker. And because of Laddy, the boys' holiday became a great success.

They were a rich family called Garaldi and lived in Rome. When they were leaving, they asked someone to take their photograph with Laddy outside the hotel. Then they got into their taxi and went to the airport. But after the taxi had left, Laddy saw bank notes lying in the road. They would never know where they had dropped the notes. They might not even notice it until they got back to Italy. They were rich people. Not like Gus and Maggie, who badly needed the money. He thought about it, then he got the bus out to the airport to give them back their money.

The Italian family all crowded round him. They shouted to everyone around them that the Irish were a generous people. They put some of the notes in Laddy's pockets. They said something again and again to him in Italian.

'They're asking you to go and stay with them in Rome,' translated someone near Laddy.

'I know,' said Laddy, 'and I'll go.' He smiled at everyone.

'I'll need to get a passport, you know,' Laddy said the next day.

'Won't you need to learn to speak Italian first,' Maggie suggested quickly, hoping he would forget the whole thing. The Italians wouldn't really expect Laddy to come to Rome. She didn't want him to be upset.

In his snooker club Laddy asked his friends about Italian lessons. A van driver, Jimmy Sullivan, said there was a woman called Signora who had come to live with them. She was starting Italian lessons up in Mountainview school.

♦

Gus and Maggie were worried that Laddy wouldn't manage in the Italian classes, but they were wrong. He loved it. He learnt the phrases that they were given each week. He greeted Italian visitors to the hotel warmly in Italian.

One evening, the Principal of the whole school came and sat beside Laddy. 'How are you?' he asked.

'*Bene, benissimo.*' Signora had told them to answer every question in Italian.

'Great, and what are you doing today?'

'We're learning parts of the body for when we get ill or have an accident in Italy. The first thing the doctor will say is *"Dov'è il dolore?"*, which means: where is the pain? and you tell him.'

Aidan Dunne had been right to fight for these classes, Tony O'Brien thought. They seemed to be a great success, and all kinds of people were coming there. Harry Kane's wife, and that man who looked a bit like a criminal. He would tell Grania about it this evening at dinner.

The parts of the body class was great fun. Tony O'Brien had to keep his hand over his face to stop laughing some of the time. But to his surprise they had learnt a lot of language and they were confident about using it. The woman was a good teacher. And these thirty people really thought that they were going on a trip to Rome. Tony O'Brien, who was a strong man, felt slightly weak at the thought.

He saw Aidan and Signora laughing over some boxes that they were changing from hospital beds into seats on a train. They were standing close together, like very good friends. Close, but not touching.

'*Dov'è il dolore?*' he said to Lorenzo.

'*Il gomito,*' shouted Laddy, holding his elbow.

◆

Things were so bad in the hotel that Gus and Maggie found it hard to help Laddy too. It would be difficult to pay all the people who worked in the hotel that week. And there was Laddy, his big face anxious, wanting them to listen to him while he practised his Italian.

And that night was the night he chose to invite Constanza in. She often drove Laddy home after the class. But she had never come in before. Gus and Maggie had just spent three hours

'Il gomito,' *shouted Laddy, holding his elbow.*

looking at their financial position. They would have to sell the hotel. And now they would have to talk politely to this woman.

But they didn't have to be polite. She told them that she was married to Harry Kane, the name on their papers and documents. She took out her chequebook and wrote a large cheque. She said the money was theirs by law. Then she left.

'Was I right to tell Constanza?' Laddy said anxiously.

'Yes, Laddy, you were right,' Gus said. His voice was very quiet but Laddy knew that he was pleased.

He must tell them how well he had done in class. 'It was great tonight. I was afraid I wouldn't remember the words but I did, all of them.'

Maggie's eyes were full of tears. They sat together, the three of them. They would always live together, as Rose had understood.

Chapter 7   Fiona

Fiona worked in the coffee shop of the city hospital. She was always bright and cheerful. Her customers needed that. Some of them were ill, some were suffering from shock.

Fiona had never been very confident about meeting men. At the age of twenty, she felt that she just wasn't good at it. Her friends, Grania and Brigid Dunne only had to go outside and they met men. Sometimes she looked at herself in the mirror. She was perhaps a little too small, and of course she had to wear glasses. But Grania and Brigid had both said she looked great and had a good figure. Were they being honest? It was so hard to know.

And then she met Barry Healy. He was young, dark, quite attractive and worked in a supermarket. Fiona liked him at once. He was visiting his mother in hospital but he didn't tell Fiona why she was there, and Fiona didn't ask.

They went to the cinema together, but it wasn't a great success. Fiona couldn't decide which film to see, which food to eat afterwards or what to say next. Barry chose everything for her. He seemed to realize quickly that he would have to make all the decisions.

It was because of her parents, of course. They were nice kind people but they had nothing to say to anyone. And now she herself had no opinions, no ideas. How did Grania and Brigid become so confident? Grania had even told her father that she was going to marry his boss. Her father had been so angry that she'd had to leave the house and stay with a friend. She must be brave, Fiona thought.

She was surprised when Barry told her that he was learning Italian up at Mountainview school.

'Oh, my best friend's father is a teacher there,' Fiona said.

Barry said he'd been to Italy for the World Cup, and hoped to go back there one day.

Fiona wanted to ask him about his mother but she decided not to. It might be too private.

He drove her home on his motorcycle.

'Goodnight, Fiona. Thank you for not asking about my mother. I didn't want to talk about it. I'll see you ... perhaps in the hospital?'

'Yes, yes, if you're passing.'

'I'll pass every day.'

◆

Barry took Fiona to a football match. There they met a dark man called Luigi. Luigi was very pleased to see Barry and they both started speaking in Italian and laughing a lot. And after the match they went to have a drink with Luigi and his girlfriend, Suzi. Suzi was beautiful, with long red hair. The men started talking about their class trip to Italy.

'Are you going to Rome?' Suzi asked Fiona.

'I'm not sure. I don't really know Barry very well yet. But if things go well, I might be able to go.'

'Start saving. It'll be great fun. Lou and I are getting married just before we go. The only problem is that the whole class will be on the trip too.'

'Well it might be easier to entertain him during the day, then.'

'Entertain him? I was expecting him to entertain me!'

Fiona was sorry she'd spoken. Of course someone like Suzi thought that way. Fiona looked at her with admiration. 'How did you become so ... you know, sure of things?' she asked. 'Was it just because you're so attractive?'

Suzi looked at her. This girl wasn't joking. 'I have no idea what I look like,' she said honestly. 'Some people like the way I look, others don't. I can't please everyone, so I decided to please myself.'

Barry had enjoyed the evening. He drove Fiona home on his motorcycle.

'Next time we'll do something that you choose,' he said. 'I'll see you tomorrow because I'm taking my mother home, but then it may be a few days until we can go out again ... when she's all right alone. Please don't think that I'm seeing anyone else ...,' he said anxiously.

Fiona realized that he really did like her. 'Oh, no, I understand.' And her smile lit up her whole face.

♦

The time seemed very long, although it was only a week. Then Barry came to see her again.

'Is everything all right at home?'

'No, not really.' And now Barry told her about his mother's illness. There was some problem between her and Barry's father. His father didn't stay at home much and his mother had become really ill worrying about it. She didn't have any interest in anything. She even refused to cook or eat. Her hospital stay had not helped much.

'I don't know what to do. But have you decided what you'd like to do when we go out?'

And suddenly Fiona did decide. 'I'd like to come and have supper at your house.'

'No, that wouldn't be a good idea, Fiona, not yet.'

'But your mother would have to make an effort if you were bringing me to supper. And I'd be cheerful too.'

'Well, you may be right . . .' They fixed the date.

◆

'I can't cook anything,' Barry's mother, Nessa, said.

'Of course you can, you're a great cook,' said Barry.

'Your father doesn't think so,' she said. Barry felt sad. Why couldn't his father just tell his wife that he loved her? After all, he was old now, nearly fifty.

'Well, all right, Mum, I'll try to cook something myself. We'll tell her you made it.'

'I'll do it,' said his mother. 'You couldn't feed the cat.'

And the evening went very well. Fiona bought Nessa Healy a box of chocolates and told her how nice she looked. And it was true, Barry hadn't seen his mother so full of life for weeks. The two of them talked together easily, and his mother began to relax.

At supper Fiona ate everything and said she'd love to be able to cook so well. And then she had a thought.

'*That's* what I could do,' she cried. 'Go to a cookery class. Barry was asking what I'd like to learn. But it wouldn't be easy finding a class in the middle of the term. Listen – no, but you . . .' she looked at Barry's mother.

'What is it?'

'It wouldn't be possible, would it, for you to show me, Mrs Healy? On Tuesday and Thursday when Barry's at his evening class?'

The older woman was silent for a moment. Then, 'I'd be very

pleased to teach you to cook, Fiona,' she said. 'We'll start next Tuesday with bread and cakes.'

◆

Grania had been home to see her father. It was the first time since she'd told him about her and Tony.

Her father took her into his study, and she stopped in surprise. The evening sun was coming through the window, shining on the yellow and gold colours all around the window seat. There were beautiful purple and gold curtains, and shelves of books. Light poured down on to his desk.

'Dad, it's beautiful! Dad . . .'

It was hard to say which of them moved first towards the other. Aidan put his arms around his daughter. There was no need for words.

◆

The cookery classes were a great success. Sometimes Barry's father, Dan, was there. Tall and dark, he looked a lot younger than his wife. He worked for a big farm, delivering to restaurants and hotels around the city. He was pleasant, but he seemed like someone who was passing through. He didn't seem to live there.

Mrs Healy was sure that Dan was meeting another woman. 'He works twenty-eight hours a week but he's out of here nearly twice as much,' she said.

'And who do you think she is?' Fiona asked quietly.

'I don't know but I'll find out,' said Nessa.

Fiona found it very upsetting to listen to her. But Fiona's company certainly seemed to help Mrs Healy. She had her hair coloured and cut short. She put on more attractive clothes. She looked fifty instead of seventy-five.

But nothing prepared Fiona for Mrs Healy's news. They were making a fruit cake.

'I've discovered who she is.'

'Who?'

56

'The woman, Dan's woman.'

'And who is she?' Fiona was anxious.

'She works in one of the best restaurants in Dublin. Quentin's. I followed him in a taxi on Wednesday evening when he went out in his van. We waited outside Quentin's and a woman came out. He called to her from his van. Her name's Nell.'

For a few minutes Fiona couldn't speak. What could she say? Brigid and Grania's mother, Nell Dunne, worked at the cash desk in Quentin's. This was very complicated.

◆

The Italian class was having a big party to get some money for the class trip, the *viaggio* as they called it, in the summer. Each pupil was expected to invite five other people who would pay five pounds each for the party. They had already booked the hotel in Rome. Barry had not yet asked Fiona to come on the trip, but Fiona hoped he would.

'Will Mr and Mrs Dunne be at the party?' Fiona asked.

'Oh, I'm sure they will.'

'And your father is coming?'

'Yes, he told me that he would,' said Barry happily.

Fiona began to think. With Mr and Mrs Dunne, and Mr and Mrs Healy all at the party, anything could happen. What should she do?

◆

Grania and Brigid were getting dressed for the party.

'I hope it goes well, for Dad,' said Grania. She was grateful to her father. He had walked into Tony's office, after months of not speaking to him, and offered him his hand. Tony had nearly fallen off his chair with the shock.

'Hey, Mum, hurry up. We're going in a few minutes,' Grania said.

'I'm ready.'

They looked at their mother. She had made no effort; her hair

57

was not even combed. Nell Dunne didn't really want to go. It would be boring, she thought, like everything in that school. Still, Dan wasn't free. He had to go somewhere with his son, he said.

◆

This was Nessa Healy's first evening out since she had been in hospital. She hadn't looked so well in years. There was no doubt that Fiona had been very good for her.

His father looked worried. 'What kind of people will be there, son?'

'All the people who go to the class, Dad. It'll be great.'

'And Fiona's meeting us there?' Mrs Healy wanted the support of this cheerful young girl that she had become so fond of. Fiona had made her promise not to say anything about Nell, just for one week. And Nessa Healy had agreed.

'Yes, we'll see her there,' said Barry. 'Are we ready?'

◆

Signora stood in the hall, tall and confident in a new dress, so unlike the shy woman who had come to Ireland a year ago. There were pictures all over the walls and bright coloured lights. A band was playing Italian music.

Aidan Dunne came in. 'I'll never be able to thank you enough,' he said.

'It is I who have to thank you, Aidan.'

Together they greeted everyone: Constanza with her children and their friends, Laddy with Gus and Maggie. Fiona saw Grania and Brigid come in with their mother. She was shocked. Mrs Dunne looked terrible. Good, thought Fiona. She knew that tonight she was going to tell some lies which would change people's lives. She, Fiona, the mouse. She had managed to get Nessa here, dressed up for this party. She must finish what she had begun.

The party was going well. People were drinking and dancing already. Fiona went to Nell Dunne, who was standing on her own.

'Do you remember me, Mrs Dunne?'

Mrs Dunne looked terrible.

'Oh, Fiona?'

'Yes. I've just come to tell you something about Dan, the man over there.'

'WHAT?' Nell looked to where Fiona was pointing.

'You know, he's got so many women friends. You're probably Wednesday's woman, aren't you?'

Nell looked at the well-dressed woman laughing easily with Dan. This couldn't be the dull wife he had spoken of. 'Why are you telling me this?' she asked Fiona.

'Well, he delivers flowers to where I work, you see, and he's always talking about his women. When I realized one of them was Grania and Brigid's mum, I felt a bit sick.'

'I don't believe you. You're crazy,' Mrs Dunne said.

Later, Fiona pulled Luigi off the dance floor. 'Could you do one thing for me without asking any questions?' she said.

'That's me,' Luigi said.

'Go over to that man and tell him to leave his Wednesday night lady alone if he knows what's good for him.'

'Are you sure he won't hit me?'

'No, he won't. And Luigi . . . could you pretend to be angry and dangerous?'

'I'll try,' said Luigi, who seemed to think it might be difficult.

Nell Dunne was going towards Dan. He was talking to a young, dark man with a very angry expression. Just before Nell reached him, Dan looked up and saw her. He looked at Luigi, took his wife's arm and began to dance.

The band was playing loudly. Fiona saw Nell Dunne get her coat and leave the room. Then Barry came and asked her to dance. He held her very tight. They passed Aidan, talking to Signora, and Barry's father, clearly enjoying his wife's company. There was Grania, holding Tony's arm. Fiona had been invited to their wedding. And Barry had just asked her if she would come on the *viaggio* with him.

Chapter 8 *Viaggio*

Grania sat with her father in his study the night before the *viaggio*. He had all his maps and guidebooks in front of him.

'Are you nervous about this trip?'

'A little. We want it to be as good as we all hope.'

They did not talk about the fact that Nell was not going. She had told her daughter that she had not been invited.

◆

Signora arrived first at the airport. There were forty-two people coming on the trip, including Aidan and herself.

Slowly the others began to arrive. Aidan had divided them into four groups of ten with a leader in each. When they arrived or left anywhere, the leader had to report that all were there. Everyone seemed quite happy about this.

'Imagine, Lou is a leader!' Suzi said to Signora.

'Well, he's a responsible married man now,' said Signora.

On the plane the announcements were made in English and Italian. They were pleased to hear the words and phrases that they had learnt. Aidan's eyes met Signora's. It was really happening. They were going to Rome.

Signora was sitting beside Laddy. Everything was new to him. But he was especially excited because he thought he was going to see his Italian friends, the Garaldis.

'Will they be at the airport?' he asked Signora.

'No, Lorenzo, but I've written to them. They know we're coming.'

Signora hoped the Garaldis would remember Lorenzo. She was worried because she had received no reply.

◆

The bus dropped them at the *Albergo Francobollo*. 'The Stamp Hotel,' Bill translated for them, with a smile. He was happy. Back in Ireland, he had said to Lizzie that Luigi was getting married,

Mr Dunne's daughter was getting married . . . 'I think we should get married soon, don't you?' And she had said, '*Perché non?*' . . . 'Why not?' with a big smile.

The *Albergo Francobollo* was not one of the best hotels in Rome but it gave them a big welcome. Signor and Signora Buona Sera were full of admiration for their Italian.

Connie was sharing a room with Signora. She hung her clothes up carefully on her side of the cupboard. It was years since she had stayed in a hotel room without its own bathroom. But she did not feel better than these people because she had more money. She just wanted to enjoy the plans that Signora and Aidan Dunne had made for them. Like every other member of the evening class, she felt that the relationship between Aidan and Signora was more than just a professional one. Nobody had been surprised when Aidan's wife had not joined the group.

◆

The bus trip would give them the feel of Rome, Signora said. Then they could all go back where they wanted and visit the places again. They would have a sandwich, and that evening there would be a big dinner in a restaurant near the hotel.

And when they came back, very tired from the trip, everyone had two hours' rest before dinner. Signora walked round to the restaurant to check the menu.

On the door she saw a sign: CLOSED, death in the family. Signora had no time to think of the unfortunate family. She hurried up and down the streets, looking for another restaurant. At last she found a place with the name *Catania*. It must be Sicilian, which might be lucky. Would they be able to serve a big, cheap meal to the class in an hour?

'Good evening,' she said.

The young man with dark hair looked up. '*Signora?*' he said. Then he looked at her again. '*Signora?* Is it possible?' And he came towards her, reaching out his hands. It was Alfredo, the oldest son of Mario and Gabriella.

Signora sat down suddenly. 'Alfredo, is this your restaurant?'

'No, no, Signora, I work here . . . to make money.'

'But your own hotel. Your mother's hotel. Why do you not work there?'

'My mother is dead, Signora. She became ill a month after my father was killed. My mother's brothers are managing the hotel. There is nothing for me to do there.'

'I'm so sorry,' Signora said. 'I can't tell you how sorry I am.' And suddenly it was all too much for her and she cried and cried with Mario's son beside her.

◆

The leaders were counting the heads to go to dinner. Everyone was there except for Laddy and Signora.

At that moment Signora arrived, looking a little pale, with the news that the restaurant had been changed but the price was the same. Aidan said that he would find Laddy; he would take the address of the restaurant and join them later.

Signora looked at him anxiously. 'I think I should go,' she said. 'Perhaps he's gone to find the Garaldis. He knew their address and there's nowhere else for him to go.'

'My God,' said Aidan,' I left him alone for twenty minutes and this is what happens. We'll both go.'

First they took the others to the restaurant. Then they got a taxi and arrived at the Garaldis' house. On the way Signora had told Aidan about her meeting with Alfredo. Aidan felt a little surprised at this new information about Signora's Sicilian past, but he was even more surprised when he saw the Garaldis' big, beautiful house. These were very rich people. Had Laddy really gone in here?

They were shown into a hall where they found Laddy. Laddy had suddenly forgotten all his Italian, and the Garaldis didn't understand who he was or what he wanted. Laddy's worried face lit up when he saw Signora and Aidan. Signora explained clearly and calmly who they all were and how Laddy had really believed that they expected him to visit them in Italy. She said that they would go now but that perhaps Signor Garaldi and his family would show Laddy that they remembered his kindness and honesty when he had returned their money to them. She asked them if they had not received her letter.

Signor Garaldi looked ashamed. He said that he received so many letters and he had thought that Signora's letter was just another one asking for money. He hadn't read it very well. Then he went up to Laddy, kissed him on both cheeks and said, 'Lorenzo, my friend.'

Laddy never stayed upset for long. 'Signor Garaldi,' he said and held him by the shoulders, 'my friend.'

There were more explanations and then wine was brought and little Italian cakes. When Signora said that they really must go, Signor Garaldi invited them all to come back for a drink and a celebration on the Thursday.

'There are forty-two of us,' Signora said.

'This house was built for celebrations like that.'

At the *Catania* everyone was singing a song. The waiters stood in an admiring group and then Alfredo said there was a surprise for them: a cake in the Irish colours.

'I can't thank you enough, Alfredo,' said Signora, 'for making the evening so special.'

'You can, Signora. Can you talk to me tomorrow?'

'Not tomorrow, Alfredo. Signor Dunne is giving a talk about Rome.'

'You can hear Signor Dunne any time. I have only a few days to talk to you. Please, Signora.'

'Perhaps he'll understand.' She looked over at Aidan. This talk was very important to him. But Alfredo looked very anxious. He clearly had something to tell her.

◆

And Aidan was very upset. He had been preparing the talk for weeks. But Connie promised to record it for Signora, so she could listen to it later.

'Alfredo, I hope this is important,' said Signora.

He made her a big cup of coffee and sat down beside her. 'Signora, I have to ask you to do something for me.'

Signora thought he was going to ask her for money. He could not know that she had nothing. 'There's a lot you do not know,' she began.

'I know everything, Signora. I know that my father loved you and you loved him. That you sat in that window sewing while we all grew up. I know that you behaved so well that you left when my mother asked you to.'

'You know all this?' her voice was a whisper.

'Yes, we all knew. And we were all so sad when you went away.'

'You were? Really?'

'We wanted to find you when my mother died. But we didn't even know your real name. And now God sends you into this restaurant. And now I can ask you. We want you to come home, Signora, where you belong.'

◆

They all loved Aidan's talk. And when it was finished, he answered all their questions. Afterwards they separated to eat their sandwiches. Aidan had told everyone the way back to the hotel. Then he just went to sit on a wall, sad that Signora had not come.

Aidan tried to think about all the good things that had come out of this year. He had shared his love of Italy with all these people. The classes, his talk, the whole trip had all been a great success. But it had really all happened because of Signora. And now she was back in Italy, and its magic was too strong for her. What business could she have with a waiter from Italy, even if she had known him as a child?

Fiona walked happily back to the hotel. She'd just left Barry in a very noisy bar where they were watching a football match on television. The conversation had been about the World Cup that Barry had been to in Italy. Fiona was glad that he was enjoying himself, and she had left him alone.

Passing a bar, she saw Mr Dunne, sitting on his own. His face was sad. Fiona looked at him. She knew so much. The relationship between his wife, Nell, and Barry's father was finished now, but she knew, like everyone on the *viaggio*, that he was in love with Signora. And she was not the old, shy Fiona now. She took a deep breath and went in.

'Mr Dunne, could I speak to you about something?'

'Of course you can, Fiona.'

'Mr Dunne, it's about Mrs Dunne. You see, she's been friendly, a bit too friendly actually with Barry's father. Barry's mother got very upset about it.'

'What?' Aidan looked completely shocked.

'It's finished now. It ended on the night of the party. If you remember, Mrs Dunne went home in a hurry.'

'Fiona, none of this is true.'

'It is actually. But you mustn't tell anyone. Because Barry doesn't know. And Grania and Brigid don't know. We don't want to get everyone upset about it.'

'So why are you telling me, if no one must know?'

'Because . . . I want you and Signora to be happy.'

'You're a very special girl,' Aidan said.

◆

'How was your meeting yesterday?' Aidan asked Signora the next day.

'It was interesting. Oh, and I've heard your talk. It was so good, Aidan, they all loved it.'

'I'd give you a repeat, you know that.' He was reaching for her hand but she pulled away.

'No, Aidan, please don't. You mustn't make me think . . . well, that you care about me and my future. You live with your wife and children. I've got a decision to make now.'

'They want you to go back to Sicily, don't they?'

'Yes, they do.'

'But if you go away and live in Sicily, then . . .'

'Then what?' her voice was gentle.

'Then my whole reason for living will go away too,' he said and his eyes filled with tears.

◆

The forty-two guests arrived at the Garaldis' house at five o'clock on Thursday in their best clothes.

'This is the kind of life I was born for,' Lizzie said as she walked slowly up the steps.

The Garaldis were all there and they had invited a photographer. All the guests had their photograph taken. There was wine, beer and little cakes.

At the end of the evening, Signor Garaldi gave a warm speech. He said that they had been made so welcome in Ireland, and today people had come to their house as strangers and would leave as friends.

At eleven o'clock the evening class from Mountainview were out on the streets of Rome again. Nobody felt like going home. Aidan and Signora walked hand in hand, and Signora told him all about Mario and Gabriella and her life in Annunziata. Aidan told her about Nell and how their marriage had ended now. Signora decided what she would say to Alfredo.

◆

The days passed quickly in Rome, and then they were catching the train to Florence. Next year's *viaggio*, Signora said, would be to Sicily. She and Aidan Dunne had promised Alfredo.

They sat away from the others on the train, Aidan Dunne and Signora in a world of their own.

All the guests had their photograph taken.

'We'll have to live in a small flat,' he said. 'We won't have much money.'

'I've never had any money,' Signora said honestly. 'I love you, Aidan.'

And for some reason, just at that moment, the others were all quiet, so everyone heard. And the other passengers on the train never understood why forty Irish people suddenly began shouting and singing a variety of songs in English and Italian. Or why so many of them were brushing tears away from their eyes.

ACTIVITIES

Chapters 1–2

Before you read

1 Have you, or a friend, ever attended evening classes? Was it a good experience? Why (not)?

2 Answer the questions. Find the words in *italics* in your dictionary. They are all in the story.

   a Where might someone *announce* delays to trains?

   b What does a fashion *designer* do?

   c If you *develop* your skills, do they get better?

   d In what area of English do you need to make most *effort*?

   e What qualities make a good secondary school *principal*?

   f Have you ever learnt to *sew*?

After you read

3 Answer the questions.

   a Does Aidan have a happy family life?

   b Who gets the Principal's job? Why?

   c Why is Aidan upset about this?

   d What position does Aidan get instead?

   e Who is the girl that Tony O'Brien is meeting regularly?

   f How long did Signora spend in Italy?

   g Why does she return to Ireland?

   h How does she meet Tony O'Brien?

   i Why does she go to see Aidan Dunne?

   j What interest do Aidan and Signora share?

4 Discuss why:

   a Aidan does not like Tony O'Brien.

   b Aidan decides to make the guest room into a study.

   c Grania does not tell her father who she is meeting.

   d Tony does not tell Grania that he is going to be Principal.

   e Grania is so upset at the end of chapter 1.

5 'Signora is a strong but gentle character.' Do you agree? Why (not)?

Chapters 3–4

Before you read

6 Why do young people become criminals? Is it always their fault, do you think?

7 Find these words in your dictionary.

attract   debt   lamb   motorcycle   phrase   pronounce
store   suitable   variety

   a If something *attracts* you, are you interested in it?
   b If you have *debts*, what do you need to do?
   c What animal does *lamb* come from?
   d How many wheels does a *motorcycle* have?
   e How many *phrases* do you know in Japanese?
   f Which words do English-speakers find difficult to *pronounce* in your language?
   g If you *store* things, do you throw them away?
   h If someone is an *unsuitable* parent, should they have children?
   i If there is a *variety* of activities, are they all the same?

After you read

8 Complete these sentences.
   a Lizzie will only marry Bill if . . .
   b Bill wants to work abroad because . . .
   c Bill borrows money from the bank because . . .
   d Bill believes that Lizzie's mother . . .
   e So he is surprised to learn that . . .
   f Bill feels more hopeful about the future because . . .

9 Who is speaking? What are they talking about?
   a 'Don't drink tonight. And perhaps I'll show you a good place to park the car.'
   b 'So has tonight ended?'
   c 'When you're part of this, you're always part of it.'
   d 'Why don't I just put them in a corner? You never know when you might need them.'
   e 'It's only glass, Signora, but it looks real, doesn't it?'
   f 'Why don't you leave now . . . I'll lock the doors for you.'
   g 'You can stop learning Italian, if you want.'
   h 'It's finished. There won't be any more of it.'

10 Discuss these questions.

    a Do you think Bill is right to feel more hopeful at the end of chapter 3? What do you think his future with Lizzie will be like?

    b Lou says, 'It's finished.' Do you think this is true? Why (not)?

Chapters 5–6

Before you read

11 Find these words in your dictionary.

    career   combine   director   divide   hospice   insurance
    invest   lawyer   porter   receptionist   snooker   specifically

    a Which words refer to:

        people?   a game?   a building?

    b What do these people do? Explain in your own words.

        a *career*'s advisor   an *insurance* salesman   an *investor*

    c How many things have you got if you

        combine two things?

        divide something?

    d Rewrite this sentence. Keep the same meaning but do not use the word in *italics*. 'I've saved this money *specifically* for a holiday.'

After you read

12 Are these statements true or false? Correct the false ones.

    a Connie was a warm and loving wife.

    b Harry was happy for the lawyer to divide their property between them.

    c Connie stayed with Harry because it was better for the family.

    d Connie refused to help Harry.

    e Gus and Maggie's hotel business was not a success.

13 Discuss these lines from a conversation.

    'Now, make sure he gives you money for yourself. Invest it. Then, if something goes wrong, you'll be all right.'

    a Who is speaking? Who to?

    b Why does the speaker say this?

    c Does the listener take the advice?

    d Do you think the speaker was right to give this advice?

    e Was the listener right to follow it?

14 Act the part of Gus or Maggie. Reply to Rose's words: 'You have to tell me what it is … You cannot leave this room without telling me.'

Chapters 7–8

Before you read

15 How would you like the story to end for these characters?
Aidan   Signora   Grania and Tony   Bill and Lizzie
Lou and Suzi   Laddy

16 Find these words in your dictionary. Which two can you see on a person's face?
band   cheek   expression

After you read

17 Who
  a is ill at the beginning of Chapter 7?
  b meets a woman outside Quentin's?
  c comes out of Quentin's to meet him?
  d watches from a taxi?
  e lies to Nell Dunne about Dan?
  f tells Dan to leave Nell alone?

18 Imagine that you are Signora. Describe your thoughts and feelings while you are listening to Alfredo.

Writing

19 Which character's story did you most enjoy? Explain why.

20 Imagine you are Suzi or Grania. Write about the events in the story as you experienced them.

21 Each of the characters faces difficulties of some kind. Which situations do you recognize from real life?

22 Describe the development of the relationship between Signora and Aidan. Do you think they will be happy together?

23 Write a newspaper report for the day after Harry Kane is sent to prison.

24 Do you agree that Signora's character holds the whole book together? Why (not)?

Answers for the Activities in this book are published in our free resource packs for teachers, the Penguin Readers Factsheets, or available on a separate sheet. Please write to your local Pearson Education office or to: Marketing Department, Penguin Longman Publishing, 5 Bentinck Street, London W1M 5RN.